# Dan's B

John Prater

CAMBRIDGE
UNIVERSITY PRESS

G000297326

Dan finds a big box. He opens it.

A Jack-in-the-box jumps up.
"Hello, Dan," he says.

Dan says, "I can do lots of things. I can stretch up high."

Jack says, "I can stretch up very high."

Dan says, "Well, I can run very fast."

Jack hides under the box.

Then Dan rolls round the room and

Jack walks on his hands.

Dan puts on his jacket and

Jack bends over backwards.

They both spin round and round, and

fall over!

They say, "We can both do lots
of things."

Dan says goodbye to Jack.

Mum comes in. "It's time for gym club,"
she says.